ON A
Starry
NIGHT

Illustrated by Alison Edgson

STRIPES PUBLISHING
An imprint of Little Tiger Press
1 The Coda Centre, 189 Munster Road, London SW6 6AW

A paperback original
First published in Great Britain in 2012

This collection copyright © Stripes Publishing, 2012
Stories copyright © Michael Broad, Holly Webb, Lucy Courtenay,
Elizabeth Baguley, Liss Norton, Karen Wallace, Malachy Doyle,
Caroline Pitcher, Caroline Juskus, Penny Dolan, 2012
Illustrations copyright © Alison Edgson, 2012

The right of Alison Edgson to be identified as the
illustrator of this work has been asserted by her in accordance
with the Copyright, Designs and Patents Act, 1988.

ISBN: 978-1-84715-258-9

Printed and bound in the UK.

2 4 6 8 10 9 7 5 3 1

ON A
Starry
NIGHT

An Enchanting Collection of Animal Tales

Stripes

CONTENTS

AFRAID OF THE DARK

Michael Broad

Anyu the Arctic fox cub was very excited as he watched the last sunset of the year with his mama and older brother, Atka. Anyu had been born in the summer and had only ever been out when it was light, but now winter had arrived there would be several weeks of darkness and he was about to see stars for the very first time.

"Wave goodbye to the sun," Mama whispered to Anyu, as the orange orb shimmered on the horizon. "And get ready to say hello to the stars that will keep watch over us until the days grow light again."

Anyu waved a snowy white paw as the sun slowly dropped out of sight, illuminating the winter wonderland with one last burst of orange and pink. Then the sky dimmed through shades of purple and dark blue until finally there were no colours left at all.

"Any moment now," said Mama, and they all tilted their heads and gazed upwards into the inky blackness.

"There!" said Anyu as the first star appeared.

"And there!" said Atka when he saw another.

Then, one by one, the stars flickered on all across the sky until there were far too many to count. They filled the winter night with silver lights that made the snow sparkle.

"Aren't they beautiful!" sighed Mama.

"WOW!" gasped Anyu, feeling like he could gaze at the stars forever. But when he looked around and saw how dark the world had become, he felt fearful and moved closer to his mother. "I can't see very well and feel a bit scared, Mama," he whispered.

"Your eyes will take a little while to get used to the dark and then you'll feel much braver," said his mother, nuzzling Anyu's soft white fur. "But until then I'm sure your brother won't mind looking out for you."

"But, Mama…" groaned Atka.

"No arguments," she smiled, standing up and stretching. "Now you two play nicely while I find some food. And what do we remember when we're outside alone?"

"Beware of bigger animals," the brothers chorused together.

"Good cubs," said Mama, and headed out into the night.

"You're such a quivering lemming, being afraid of the dark," said Atka. "And now

I have to look after you instead of playing with my friends."

"I don't need to be looked after," Anyu said uncertainly.

"Well, you can't be out here on your own now it's dark," sighed Atka. "But I'm not sure even *I* can stop you getting gobbled up by the Snow Monster."

"What's the S-s-snow M-m-monster?" stammered Anyu.

"He's a huge beast that walks on two legs, with a big hairy face and huge claws and teeth!" whispered Atka in a low voice. "And he likes nothing more than to eat little fox cubs for dinner!"

"You're making it up," said Anyu.

"No, I'm not," said Atka.

"Then how come I've never seen him?" Anyu frowned.

"The stars aren't the only ones that sleep during the daylight," said Atka, looking around as if checking for big hairy beasts. "The Snow Monster only ever hunts when it's dark. Everyone knows that."

"Why?" asked Anyu.

"Because that's when little fox cubs can't see very well," said Atka, moving behind his brother. "He creeps up behind them and before they even know what's happening…"

"EEEEK!" yelped Anyu as Atka tugged his tail, making him jump high in the air in fright. The little fox cub landed on the snow and then scampered off into the den.

For the next few days Anyu stayed in the den while Atka went out with his friends. Mama tried to encourage Anyu to go too, but he always made excuses. And when Atka returned, he told his little brother tales about close encounters with the Snow Monster.

"Oh, he nearly got me tonight!" said Atka, rearing up on his hind legs and staggering around. "That hairy beast came bounding after me on two long legs, leaping over the snowdrifts, his eyes glowing red, snarling and drooling through his enormous jaws!"

"How did you get away?" gasped Anyu.

"Because I'm big and brave and can see in the dark," said Atka, chasing his little brother around. "Had I been a quivering lemming like you, I think he would have gobbled me up right there and then!"

Atka's stories grew more incredible as each dark day passed, until one evening when his brother went out, Anyu's mother asked why he wasn't going, too. The cub had run out of excuses so he told his mama all about the Snow Monster, describing the creature's terrifying appearance.

"Goodness me, I've never seen anything that looks like that," said Mama, and then smiled kindly at Anyu. "I think naughty Atka has been teasing you with

make-believe monsters."

Realizing that his brother had tricked him and feeling foolish for believing him, the little fox cub plucked up his courage, crept along the tunnel to the entrance of the den and peeped outside. Even if the monster was made up, there were other dangers and he was still afraid of the dark. But Anyu wanted to prove to Atka and himself that he could brave the darkness alone.

First he poked out his ears and listened carefully for footfalls in the snow. Then he lifted his nose and twitched it, sniffing the chilly air for any unusual scents, and then he opened his eyes wide and looked all around. Anyu still couldn't see well in the darkness and wanted to run back to Mama, but he also didn't want to be a quivering lemming. So one paw at a time, the little fox stepped all the way out of the den.

Anyu took a step further, and then another and another, and as he padded through the snow the starlight began to reveal different shapes. A snowy owl swooped down from the sky, silver light edging its wings. An Arctic hare bounded past, its furry feet spraying glistening snowflakes. And, in the distance, Anyu made out a patch of darkness that was somehow darker than everything else. The little fox did not know what it was, but it looked like a group of trees with bare branches had sprung up where there had been no trees before. Thinking this was very strange, he decided to be brave and explore.

It was only when he got close that Anyu realized the trees were moving, and not simply bending in the breeze. They were walking about and making crunching sounds on the snow!

Anyu froze and squinted, and just then a shooting star offered enough light for him to see that the trees were actually a small herd of reindeer with tall antlers. Anyu sighed with relief, but the shuffling deer hooves meant he didn't hear another creature moving through the herd until it loomed out of the darkness, huge and tall and walking upright on two legs.

"The Snow Monster!" gasped Anyu, and froze again.

The little fox cub was too frightened to

run in case the beast saw him and gave chase, so he kept still and hoped he would not be spotted.

The creature was large and red, with bushy white hair on his head and a big round belly. He was stomping around, shaking out turnips from a brown sack to feed the reindeer herd.

He's fattening them up to eat, thought Anyu and swallowed hard.

Just then, the creature turned away and the fox cub saw his chance. He scampered off, heart pounding as he raced across the snow, and didn't stop until he was back inside the den.

"Mama, I saw the Snow Monster!" he panted, trying to catch his breath. "He was

huge and hairy and on two legs and everything!"

"Are you sure?" his mother replied calmly.

"Yes, he was feeding the reindeer!" Anyu added.

"That doesn't sound like something a monster would do," said Mama.

"He probably eats them when they grow fat enough," he gasped. "I thought he was going to gobble me up!"

"Well, I'm glad he didn't," she smiled, nuzzling Anyu. "Now, I think it's time for one imaginative little cub to get some sleep."

Anyu could tell Mama didn't believe him or she would have been really worried. But he knew someone who would *have* to believe him. Yet though he tried to stay awake until Atka came home, the little cub was so exhausted that he fell fast asleep.

The following day Anyu told his brother all about venturing out alone and his close encounter with the Snow Monster.

"You can't fool me, little quivering lemming," teased Atka. "You probably just saw your own shadow, got scared and ran away!"

"No, I really saw him," Anyu persisted. "He was big and hairy, just like you said!"

"Look, there's no such thing as the Snow Monster," Atka sighed. "I made him up just to frighten you, so I wouldn't have to take you everywhere with me."

"But I saw him!" Anyu pleaded. "And if

you come out with me at the same time tonight, I'll prove it."

Atka felt a little bad about scaring his younger brother so much that he'd started imagining things. And their mother had had words with him the night before. So he agreed to come out with Anyu that evening.

"I'm sure the Snow Monster is fattening the reindeer up to eat," said Anyu, as they trotted across the snow towards the herd. "And he had a very big belly, so he probably eats foxes, too!"

When the brothers finally arrived, the herd was still there and seemed more restless than the night before. So the Arctic fox cubs stopped a little distance away.

"Where is he, then?" asked Atka.

"There!" said Anyu, just as the big hairy beast lit a lantern and began to tether seven of the reindeer together with ropes and bells. "Oh, he must be really hungry tonight if he's taking so many!"

Anyu was feeling quite confident having his big brave brother with him. But when he turned round and saw the terrified look on Atka's face, he realized his brother wasn't quite as brave as he'd thought.

"The S-s-snow M-m-monster!" Atka babbled, and with a loud yelp he ran away, leaving the little cub all alone.

When Anyu looked back at the reindeer he saw the Snow Monster stomping towards him, holding his lantern high. The beast must have heard his brother's yelp

and was coming to investigate. Within moments he was standing over the tiny trembling fox.

"Don't worry, little one," he said. "I won't hurt you."

Anyu squinted up into the light and saw that the creature had a face in the middle of all that white hair. But it wasn't a frightening face, it was a jolly pink face with bright rosy cheeks, and it was smiling kindly at him.

"It must be scary when you can't see all that's around you," he said, scratching his beard thoughtfully. "I wonder…"

The creature went back to the seven reindeer that were tethered to a sleigh, hung the lantern on the side and rummaged around inside a large brown sack. Anyu thought he might be fetching him a turnip, but instead he returned with something wrapped in colourful paper and placed it in front of the cub.

"Happy Christmas, Anyu," he said.

Anyu sniffed the small, thin package and then tore at the paper with his teeth until the contents rolled out in front of him. The cub had no idea what it was until the Snow Monster reached down and showed him,

before returning to the sleigh. He clambered into the seat and shook the reins, making the bells jingle merrily.

The Arctic fox cub gazed, wide-eyed, as the whole sleigh lit up as if by magic. Then the reindeer galloped through the snow and took to the air in a trail of light that was brighter than the stars in the sky.

Back in the den, Atka was telling Mama about his terrifying encounter with the Snow Monster. Suddenly he saw a bright light appear in the den's snowy entrance, followed by a shadow that grew bigger as it moved along the tunnel wall.

"EEEEK!" yelped Atka, thinking the

monster had eaten his little brother and was now looking for him!

He quickly hid behind Mama as the shadow drew closer, then all at once it shrank down. Anyu stepped into the den with a big smile on his face and something in his mouth.

"Look what the Snow Monster gave me!" he exclaimed through his teeth, waving around a brand-new torch. "It lights everything up just like sunshine!"

THE CHRISTMAS VISITOR

Holly Webb

"Lucy! Lucy!"

Lucy looked up from her book. She was huddled into the little armchair in the corner of the living room, next to the radiator, and she had a fleecy blanket wrapped round her. It was freezing, even inside the house. Everyone said it was going to snow soon, and she wished it would. At the moment, the days were just cold and dark. It wasn't making the holidays feel very Christmassy.

The living-room door slammed open, and her little brother stood there, panting. He was practically round. When he'd said he wanted to go and play in the garden, Mum had insisted on him wearing a fleece under his big coat, and two scarves.

"What is it? Is it snowing?" Lucy asked hopefully, turning to peer out of the window. But the sky was still a dark streaky grey, and no snow was falling.

"No. I've found something. Come and see!" Sam was so excited, he was actually dancing up and down.

"Outside?" Lucy shuddered. "No, thank you."

"You have to!" Sam trundled up to her armchair, snatching the book and snapping

it closed. "Come on, Lucy, he might go! You'll be sorry if you miss him!"

Lucy frowned. "Miss who? Oh, Sam, it's not another spider, is it? Ha-ha, very funny. Lucy doesn't like spiders. Old joke."

Sam shook his head. "No. Actually, I think he might eat spiders. So you should really like him. Come on!"

"A frog?" Lucy asked doubtfully. She couldn't think of anything else that might eat spiders. Maybe a bird…

"Of course not a frog!" Sam sighed. "I'm going back out, I want to watch him." He stomped away, and Lucy stared after him. He had sounded very excited…

Shaking her head, she hurried into the hallway to find her coat and her snowboots.

Then she went out of the back door, rubbing her gloved hands together as the cold air bit into her.

The frost was still thick and silvery on the grass, even though it was the middle of the afternoon. And there was actually an icicle hanging off the dripping garden tap! What on earth was she doing out here, instead of snuggled up in the warm?

"You came! He's here, Lucy, look!" Sam turned round from the little wooden shelter by the garden shed. Dad had made it, to store the logs for the wood-burning stove. Next to the logs was a tatty old wicker basket, full of thin twigs and dry leaves for kindling.

"What is it?" Lucy stayed a safe distance away. She really didn't like fetching logs for

the stove. She always seemed to get jumped on by the world's most enormous spiders. They liked the dry, woody little space.

"I'm not quite sure!" Sam sounded excited, but then he added, in a worried sort of voice, "But whatever animal he is, I don't think he's very well, Lucy. He's a bit wobbly."

Forgetting about the spiders, Lucy hurried over. Sam was crouched down in front of the wood store, and at his feet was a brownish, spiky ball.

"A hedgehog!" Lucy leaned down to look closer, and saw a soft little brown snout, and two dark, glittering eyes. The hedgehog was waving his nose from side to side, as though he was confused.

"Shouldn't he be asleep?" Lucy said.

"Don't hedgehogs hibernate?"

Sam looked up at her, frowning. He didn't know what hibernate meant.

"They sleep through the cold winter. Because there isn't much for them to eat, I think," said Lucy. "No slugs around when it's snowing."

"They eat slugs?" Sam looked disgusted. "Yuck!" Then his face crumpled. "But I woke him up! I didn't mean to, but I wanted to build a track for my cars with the wood, and I pulled the basket out and he fell out of it." He was starting to cry. "Will he be OK? It's really cold."

Lucy nodded worriedly. "I hope so... I don't know. We have to get him to go back to sleep in the warm." She put her arm round Sam's shoulders – she could feel them heaving, even through his layers of clothes. "It's OK. It's not your fault, Sam. We'd have woken him getting the logs for the stove, sooner or later. We'll find out what to do. I'll go and ask Mum if she knows about hedgehogs."

"I'll stay here and look after him," Sam sniffed.

Lucy glanced at the hedgehog. He didn't look as though he was about to wander off. He still seemed very dopey. "But don't touch him, OK? I don't think he'll like it."

Sam nodded seriously.

As Lucy headed back to the house, the back door banged in the next garden, and there was a rush of scampering paws, and happy barking.

Lucy gulped. Sukey and Billy! They were gorgeous spaniels, but they were a nightmare for chasing cats, and she was pretty sure they'd chase a hedgehog, too. Even with all those prickles... She needed to get that hedgehog tucked up safe and warm again as soon as possible.

She raced across the garden, calling, "Mum! Mum!"

"What's the matter?" Her mum opened the kitchen door. "Are you OK? What were you doing outside?"

"A hedgehog," Lucy gasped. "Sam woke

him up by accident. We need to get him to go back to bed. How do we do it?"

Her mum blinked. "No idea. But I bet we can find a website to tell us." She hurried down the hall and turned on her computer in the little alcove under the stairs. "Hedgehogs… Disturbed hibernation?"

Lucy nodded. "That sounds right. He was in the wood store, in the kindling basket."

"OK." Mum showed Lucy the website she'd found and they read it together. "It says we need to feed him something – we don't have cat food," said Mum. "But there's a bit of roast chicken left from yesterday. See if you can find it in the fridge."

Lucy dashed back to the kitchen. "Got it! Anything else?"

"Oh, peanut butter, we've got that!" Mum called.

Lucy found the jar, and added a big dollop of crunchy peanut butter to the saucer with the leftover chicken on it. She wrinkled her nose. It looked like a bit of a weird combination.

Mum came in to join Lucy. "And raisins, apparently."

"Raisins? Really? OK…" Lucy found some and scattered them artistically over the top. "Did you find out anything else?"

"Only that he might want to go and find somewhere else to sleep, now that he's been disturbed," Mum told her.

"Oh no… He doesn't look like he's up to that, Mum. And I'm worried about him going next door — what about Sukey and Billy?"

Mum nodded. "I see what you mean. Well, if we put really nice food down for him, maybe he'll stay put, and go back to his old bed."

Lucy sighed. "It's the best we can do, isn't it? And maybe warn Mara next door to watch out for him whenever she lets Sukey and Billy out. Do you think that's enough food?"

Mum smiled. "Enough for a hedgehog Christmas party. Come on."

"He's still here," Sam called in a sort of loud whisper as he saw Mum and Lucy coming down the garden path.

"It's even colder now it's getting dark." Lucy shivered. "Poor hedgehog."

The hedgehog was hunched up in front of the wood store, looking sleepy. But he heard them coming and looked up, backing away from them a little.

"It's OK," Lucy whispered, putting the food down. She put it close to the pile of logs, hoping that he'd eat, and then go back and curl up behind them. She glanced round at Mum. "If he's sleeping here, we'll have to use some different wood for the stove! Or we'll keep waking him up!"

Mum nodded. "It's OK. We can put

some logs in the garage instead."

"Look! He's going to eat it!" Sam said excitedly, and then clapped his hand over his mouth as the hedgehog looked up from the peanut butter again. "Sorry!" he whispered.

Lucy giggled. "He's got it on his nose!"

He had. He was obviously hungry – he wolfed the peanut butter down with loud grunts, and then started on the chicken.

"We need to make sure he's cosy..." Lucy muttered. And then she grinned. "Back in a minute!" She dashed in to the house, and then came back out to the garden, trailing a long, pink scarf.

"What's that for?" Mum asked, frowning.

"To help him keep warm! It said on the website about them needing extra warmth in their nests when it's really cold, didn't it? It's OK, Mum. It's the one Gran knitted me last Christmas. You know she's knitting another one for this year, she always does!"

Mum sighed. "You're right. Orange and purple stripes, this year's one."

Lucy made a face. "Well, then I think

it's OK to give this one to a good cause, don't you?" She picked out a few of the logs from one side of the wood store, and she and Sam arranged them into a sort of pyramid behind the kindling basket, making sure it was really solid. They didn't want the logs to fall on their hedgehog. Then she tucked in the scarf to make a snuggly nest underneath.

"Let's step back a bit," Mum suggested. "If he does want to go in, he might not do it when he knows we're watching."

They headed a safe distance away, peering round the corner of Sam's slide.

The hedgehog licked the plate clean of the last chickeny bits, and sniffed the air thoughtfully.

Lucy laughed. "He looks like Grandad, deciding which armchair to sleep in after Sunday lunch! He really does!"

It was true. The hedgehog looked very full, and very sleepy. If he'd had a knitted waistcoat on (Gran liked to knit those, too) he would have been a dead ringer for Grandad. He wandered a few steps towards the wood store, and gave Lucy and Sam's new nest a cautious sniff.

"He likes it!" Sam whispered excitedly as the hedgehog stepped a little closer.

And he did. He went all the way in, padding down the scarf, and making sleepy little snuffling noises.

"We should leave him to go to sleep," Lucy murmured.

"Can we go and see him later?" Sam asked hopefully as they headed back to the house. "Can we make sure he's OK?"

Mum shook her head. "We probably shouldn't. He needs to get back to sleep."

Lucy frowned. "It's only two days till Christmas. Maybe we could go and see him again on Christmas morning? If we promise to leave him alone till then?"

Sam sighed. "I suppose so." Then he turned round, beaming. "Lucy, look!" He pointed up at the sky, which was a dark purply blue now, with a few stars glittering.

Fat snowflakes were mixing with the stars, and twirling down towards them. Lucy laughed, and stretched out her hands, catching the sparkling flakes. Then she gave Sam a hug. "It's lucky you found him when you did, Sam. What if Dad had gone to get some logs, and the hedgehog had woken up and gone wandering out in a snowstorm? Now we know to keep him safe."

Sam nodded. "We can look after him – he's our special Christmas visitor!"

STAR BEAR

Lucy Courtenay

It was a bitter, bright winter's night. The moon was full and fat and glowing. Thousands of stars shone on the black velvet of the sky like ropes of diamonds, tumbled and tangled together.

The light was so bright that it broke through the canopy of the deep, dark woods. It flowed between the thick tree trunks. It whispered along the mossy ground until it came to the dark mouth of a bears' winter den.

Meska the bear cub made her bed as comfortable as she could. She closed her eyes. She breathed slowly. But the bright light pouring into the den made it impossible to go to sleep.

"The stars are so bright tonight, Grandmother," Meska grumbled. She wriggled and tossed and turned and wriggled some more. "I can't sleep, even though winter's here."

"The stars shine extra brightly when they want to tell us a story," Grandmother replied.

Meska didn't realize the stars could talk. Suddenly, she wanted to know what they were saying. "What story?" she asked.

"I thought you wanted to go to sleep," said Grandmother.

"Maybe a story will help," said Meska.

"It's a very, very old story," said Grandmother. She settled in close and held Meska with warm paws. "My grandmother told it to me on a night just as bright as this one. I expect her grandmother told her, too. The story goes all the way back to when the moon was young, and the stars were as new and  bright as the silver scales on a freshly caught fish."

"Is it a happy story?" asked Meska.

"It's happy *and* sad," said Grandmother.
"Like all the best stories."

"But is there a happy ending?"

"Of course!" said Grandmother.

Meska snuggled into her grandmother's
fur, in the dappled moonlight that fell on
the earth floor of the den. "I'm listening,"
she said.

Grandmother began.

*Long ago, humans made wars and crowned
themselves kings and queens, built palaces, and
hunted us bears in the forests with bows and
spears. They did all these things because they
thought that they ruled the earth. But they
were wrong. Way up in the sky, the gods were
in charge. And the king of the gods was Zeus.*

Zeus wasn't a kind king. He was big and fierce and took what he wanted the minute he wanted it. If he was in a good mood he made something nice happen, like a cub's first growl or a bright and beautiful rainbow. But if he was in a bad mood, he made trouble. Earthquakes when he stamped his feet. Thunderstorms when he lost his temper and shook his great lightning spear. His wife Hera didn't like him, and Zeus didn't like Hera either. They weren't the happiest king and queen that ever lived.

"Is this the sad bit?" checked Meska.

"Cuddle up and keep listening," said Grandmother.

Down on earth there was a beautiful girl called Callisto. Callisto lived in the forest with a group of friends, who promised each other that they would never fall in love, get married or have children. The women hunted in the forest and they climbed the trees. They played all day and all night, and life was good.

"We're happy just as we are!" they said as they bathed in the forest pools and threaded flowers through each other's long hair.

"I love you all," said Artemis, the oldest and most important woman in the group. She smiled as Callisto and the others danced in the moonlight. "I hope that we stay this way forever."

"What's this got to do with the stars?" asked Meska with a yawn.

Grandmother stroked Meska's brown fur. "Artemis was Zeus's daughter, the goddess of the moon. And the stars will have their moment, I promise."

Up in the skies, Zeus looked down at the earth and saw Callisto dancing by a woodland pool. He instantly fell in love. And when Hera wasn't looking, he went to visit Callisto.

"You are the most beautiful girl I have ever seen," he told her.

Callisto blushed and laughed and danced for Zeus.

Gods are irresistible when they want to be.

Callisto broke all her promises to her friends and fell in love with Zeus. And very soon, she found that she was going to have a baby.

Callisto's friends were angry that she'd broken her promises. But Artemis was furious. The trees in the wood shook and trembled at her wrath. She wasn't Zeus's daughter for nothing.

"What have you done?" Artemis raged. "You have broken my heart and lied to us all. You cannot stay here any more. Leave us and never come back."

Callisto wept and pleaded with Artemis. "Let me stay!" she cried. "I have nowhere else to go."

But Artemis turned her back and never looked at Callisto again.

"That *is* sad," said Meska. She got more comfortable on her bed of grass and leaves. "I thought Artemis was Callisto's friend."

"Callisto thought the same," said Grandmother. "But she was wrong. Artemis had her father's unkind nature."

Meska gave another huge yawn. "You haven't mentioned the stars yet, Grandmother," she said sleepily.

"I know," said Grandmother. "Because there is a very important part of the story still to come."

Callisto left her friends and made a lonely place for herself in the woods. When she had her baby — a bright-eyed boy — she named him Arcas, and she loved him very much.

But Callisto's troubles weren't over. As she cuddled her baby boy and covered his dark curly head with kisses, Zeus's jealous wife Hera was hunting Callisto down.

"I will have my revenge on the girl who stole my husband's heart," she swore. And the heavens trembled to hear it.

Hera tore up forests and emptied rivers in her vengeful quest. And when she found her, Hera snapped her cold fingers and turned Callisto into a bear.

Meska opened her eyes with surprise. "A bear like me?" she said with delight.

"A little bigger," said Grandmother. "But yes. A bear like you."

"Did she turn Callisto's baby boy into a cub?"

Grandmother looked serious. "No," she said. "And that is the sad part."

Callisto tried to care for Arcas, but hunters came into the forest and chased her away from her baby. There was no time for goodbyes. For sixteen long years, Callisto roamed the woods as a bear, hunted by humans and mourning the loss of her son. Was he safe? Had he grown up strong and tall? Did he ever think of his mother?

Or did he think Callisto had abandoned him because she didn't love him any more? It was a difficult life for a bear who had once been human, for she was still full of human feelings. Callisto was lonely and tired and very frightened for her son.

One day, Callisto was wandering through a part of the forest she'd never visited before. The trees were lush and the fruit was ripe. Although she didn't know it, the wood belonged to Zeus himself.

As she pulled the berries from a ripe raspberry bush with her large brown paws, a young man with dark curly hair sprang out from behind the trees and levelled his spear at her. Callisto froze as she recognized him. It was her son, Arcas.

"I will kill you, bear!" threatened Arcas.

He lifted his spear to his shoulder and threw it. Callisto could do nothing to stop him.

"No, Grandmother!" Meska was trembling with fear. "Don't say that Arcas killed her. Please. Hurry to the happy ending!"

Grandmother smiled.

At that very same moment, Zeus was walking

in his wood. As he came into the clearing, he knew at once that the bear was Callisto, and the boy was her son. He knew because he was a god, and gods know everything. And because Arcas was half god himself, he suddenly knew it, too.

"Mother!" he cried in terror, as his spear flew towards Callisto's heart.

Zeus had loved Callisto once. Love is stronger than anything, even the cruellest of gods. And so he called out a word so wild and magical that before Arcas's despairing eyes, Callisto began to change. Her fur whitened and glimmered as her heart, her ears, her whole body turned from fur and flesh to white and shining stars. The spear clattered harmlessly to the ground as Callisto

the star bear leaped into the sky.

Arcas fell to his knees, filled with terrible sadness. He had found his mother and lost her again in the wink of a star.

Zeus was not a kind god, as I have said. But the boy's unhappiness touched him, and so Zeus sent him into the sky as well. Now two star bears, mother and son, twirl and dance together in the night skies forever.

Meska smiled and relaxed as Grandmother finished the story. Her eyes began to flutter shut. "That's nice," she mumbled. She turned over on her side with a sigh. "Callisto and Arcas, together again. Shining..."

Grandmother padded to the entrance of

the den. Two bears, one great and one small, shimmered together in the deep black sky.

"Sleep well, little Meska," said Grandmother as the cub drifted at last into her long winter sleep. "And dream of stars."

A STAR IN THE DARKNESS

Elizabeth Baguley

Josh stood on the back doorstep of Granfer's cottage. The winter's afternoon had thickened into night. There wasn't a glimmer of brightness anywhere, apart from the ghost-light cast by the snow. There were no stars, just a sky full of falling flakes blown by a cruel wind.

You can do it, Josh told himself. After all, he only needed to go to the shed to get more wood for the fire. It was really important not to let it go out. Granfer needed to be kept warm because of his cough. Also, because of the snow, the electricity had been cut off and the burning logs gave the only light in the house. But the shed was right at the end of the yard, almost on the moor itself. Granfer had once told Josh about the wild beast that people said lived out there. It was supposed to be a large cat, a bit like a panther – though Granfer said that was just a story. Nevertheless, Josh couldn't get it out of his head, and now he had to go down the garden by himself in all this snow and darkness.

Could it really be Christmas Eve? That morning Dad had suddenly announced that

they had to visit Granfer because he hadn't been very well and Josh had felt horribly disappointed. He'd wanted to stay at home, with its twinkly fairy lights and candles, decorating the Christmas cake and putting out the stockings, but Dad's no-nonsense voice told him that he didn't have much choice.

The weather was dreadful, too. By the time they'd reached Granfer's cottage, snow was falling so thickly that it was hard to tell where the sky ended and the moor began. The car had slid dangerously on the hill up to the cottage so they'd parked it and walked. How awful it would be if they got snowed in and couldn't get home for Christmas Day.

Inside the cottage, it was pretty glum too.

Granfer hadn't been able to get out, and when Mum and Josh had looked in the pantry, all they could find were a few old tins of this and that, a biscuit, half a bottle of milk and some sliced bread.

"We'll have to walk to the village shop," Mum had said to Dad. "You stay here and keep Granfer company, Josh." That had been ages ago and they still weren't back.

Normally, Josh wouldn't have minded. Granfer was old, but he was really good fun. He had a brilliant collection of bird skeletons and owl pellets, and they'd often gone out together looking for wildlife. One day, they'd gone otter-spotting, which was magical. Granfer had taught Josh to keep perfectly still and wait. Sure enough, after

a long time, the smooth head of an otter had broken the surface of the water and made Josh's heart drum in his chest.

This time, though, everything was different. Granfer had just sat by the fire with a blanket over his knees and when Josh had asked him about the wild animals, Granfer had said, "I don't really know, lad. I've not been able to get outside." Eventually, he'd dropped off to sleep. It was as if the snow had turned off the electricity inside Granfer, too. His eyes had lost their spark and he hadn't spoken again until the fire had almost burned out.

"Could you get some wood from the shed, lad?" he'd asked, half waking from his doze.

Which was why Josh was here, standing

on the doorstep. The familiar, cluttery garden with its twisty trees and rustly bushes, bird tables and heaps of twiggy stuff had been changed by the snow. Its lumps and bumps might be hiding anything – maybe even a wild beast.

Josh took a deep breath and plunged into the blizzard. Several times he tripped in the darkness, but eventually he reached the shed and got the key into the lock. Now there were only the logs to find and soon he'd be back, safe in the house. There really was nothing to be afraid of.

So what was that noise coming from the shed?

Growling. Long, low growling from behind the door.

Josh was shaking, and it wasn't just from the cold. What should he do? For a while, he stood listening. No sound but the snow pattering on dried leaves.

Had he really heard anything at all? Or was it just the sound of the wind mixed up with his imaginings of wild beasts on the moor?

Yes, it was only that. *You've just got to open the door, grab the firewood, run back,* Josh told himself. He turned the key. All quiet inside. Now he was twisting the door handle and opening it a crack. Easy. But...

What was that? Something dark sprang straight towards Josh. It yowled. He stumbled away from the shed, and landed on his back in the snow. Above him, in a holly tree, a creature crouched, its eyes a vivid yellow, luminous and alien.

And completely, utterly amazing.

Shadowy against the white snow in the tree, a small, black, furry, hissing animal.

A feral cat, that's what it was. Granfer had told him about them – cats that belonged to no one, living wild on the moor.

But it was horribly thin. How long had it been locked in the shed? When had it last eaten anything? There wouldn't be much to hunt in this weather. What if it starved? He had to do something.

Gently, gently, Josh got up and crept back to the house. Crossing his fingers that the cat wouldn't run away while he was gone, he carefully opened the back door and slid inside.

Should he wake Granfer? There wasn't time. He rushed to the pantry. Good – one of the old tins had sardines in it. He put them in a dish and carried them quietly down the garden.

The cat was still in the tree.

Slowly, as if he were weightless, Josh laid

the dish down and waited. So did the cat.
Josh waited some more. His knees ached,
but he remembered the otter days with
Granfer and knew that if he moved now he
would frighten the cat away. *Come on, puss,*
he willed.

At last, drawn by the strong smell of
fish, the cat made a sudden leap and landed
in the snow, close enough to
touch. Warily it edged
towards the dish,
sniffed — and
began to eat.
Don't breathe!

The cat was quite small — probably a
female, then. Her fur was tatty and hardly
hid how bony she was. For all her growling

in the shed, as she ate ravenously she looked like any ordinary pet. Granfer said that sometimes, if you were patient, you could tame a feral cat. "You just need to love them," he'd told Josh.

A gust of wind blew a whirlwind of leaves behind the jumpy animal. Startled, she twisted away from the dish and sprang back up the holly tree. At least she'd eaten some of the food. Josh picked up the dish and turned to go inside, bursting to tell Granfer. But first he had to get the wood — the old man would be getting cold.

He was soon inside, juggling an armful of logs and the dish, which slipped from his hand and clanged on to the floor, spilling the remains of the sardines. The old man stirred. "Sorry it took so long, Granfer," Josh said. "But there was a cat in the woodshed."

"A cat?" Granfer mumbled, still half asleep.

"She was starving," said Josh, and quickly told his story. More alert now, Granfer sent him to see if she was still there, hoping that somehow they'd be able to tempt her inside. Josh opened the back door and squinted at the tree, but the cat had gone. The wind moaned. *Such a little cat*, thought Josh, *to be out there in the cold*. Sighing, he was about to go back inside when a shadow moved on the snow. Moved and stopped, one paw raised.

Almost as if he were a mirror, Josh stopped, too. The dropped sardines were lying just inside the door and the cat's eyes were fixed on them.

"Move gently away," Granfer whispered. He got up from his chair and steered Josh behind the living room door where they could hide. Granfer seemed suddenly to have come to life. It was as though someone had turned the switch on inside him again. It made his eyes sort of smile. No wonder. The shadow was coming into the unlit hall, blending with the darkness there.

A nod from Granfer told Josh to close the back door. Watchfully, the cat ventured step by step towards the sardine scraps — then began to eat. Josh and Granfer tiptoed away and sat by the fire so that she wasn't disturbed.

"I wish she'd stay here," whispered Josh. "So that we could look after her. Do you think she will?"

"She might," Granfer replied. "Go and put my blanket down here by the fire while she's eating. Let's see if she'll settle on it."

Josh carefully arranged the blanket into a bundle and they sat like statues. Having licked the dish clean, the little cat made cautiously for the warm, woolly pile and tapped it with a soft paw. Then she circled, flattening it, before sitting down comfortably to wash her ears.

"Do you think I could stroke her?" asked Josh.

"Not yet," said Granfer. "Maybe if you were very patient. Pity you've got to go home tonight."

Suddenly, Josh didn't want to go home at all.

So when Mum and Dad came back and broke it to Josh that the roads were so icy that they'd have to stay the night, Josh felt something flutter in his chest. Now he'd have time to be very patient indeed.

Somehow, finding the cat had made everything brighter. The logs in the hearth were blazing and Granfer found an old storm lantern to hang in the kitchen. Mum lit candles and Dad dragged in a holly bough for a Christmas tree, which they decorated with tinfoil tinsel made by Josh.

"All we need now is a star," said Dad.

Granfer nodded over towards the cat. In the firelight, her eyes glowed golden against her midnight black fur. "I reckon we've got one, don't you, lad?" asked Granfer.

"Yes, Granfer," said Josh, smiling. "I reckon we have."

A PRESENT
FOR
EVERYONE

Liss Norton

"I'm bored!" sighed Jemima Wren. It was a winter's day in the Land of Cloudy Skies, and she was perched in a tree looking out at the snowy ground and grey sky.

"Me, too," tweeted her friend Gus Goldfinch. He landed on a twig nearby, his yellow-striped wings flashing, and dislodged a shower of snow.

Just then, Jemima spotted something – a big, grey, flappy something, flying through the cloudy sky. It was heading their way.

"What's that?" she asked, fluttering quickly to the top of the tree to see better. She was the tiniest bird in the whole wood, with brown feathers and darker brown stripes on her wings and tail, but she wasn't scared of anything.

She landed on the topmost twig where she had a good view of the sky. "Hey, everyone!" she called excitedly, recognizing the huge, grey bird. "Herbie's home!"

Herbie Heron had gone exploring weeks ago and now he was back. Jemima knew he'd have stories to tell and she could hardly wait to hear them. They were just what the woodland animals and birds needed to cheer them up on a wintry afternoon.

"Good old Herbie!" Gus chirped.

Jemima flew quickly to the pond to wait for Herbie to arrive. Gus and her other friends, Isabella Blackbird, Suki Starling and Rosa and Ralph, the Rook twins, raced after her. "Hooray for Herbie!" they twittered.

Down on the ground, the animals were excited, too. "Let's go and meet him!" cried Willow Rabbit.

By the time Herbie reached the pond, all the birds and animals were waiting. "Welcome home, Herbie," they called.

"It's good to be back," Herbie replied.

"Where have you been?" asked Jemima. "And what have you seen?"

"Marvels!" said Herbie, folding his massive wings. "I've been to a place where there are no clouds."

"That's impossible!" everyone gasped in amazement. The sky was always full of thick, grey clouds where they lived.

"No, it's not," said Herbie. "The sky's clear and blue all day there, and the sun shines, making everything warm and bright." He lifted one foot to scratch his feathery tummy. "And at night the moon comes up. And the stars..." He gazed round at them, his eyes shining. "Oh, you should see the stars! They're silver and glittery.

The most beautiful things in the whole world!"

Jemima could hardly believe what she was hearing. A land without clouds, where beautiful stars glittered at night? She wished with all her might that the clouds would disappear and that she could see stars, too.

She looked up at the sky. The grey clouds were a long way above her, but perhaps the sun, moon and stars were hidden behind them. If she flew very, very high she might be able to reach them. "I'm going to fly right up through the clouds," she said, "so I can see stars, too." She spread her wings.

"Don't, Jemima! The clouds are too high for a tiny bird like you," warned Rosa.

"And you haven't heard all my news yet," said Herbie.

Jemima folded her wings again.

"King Ermine and Queen Ruby have a new baby daughter," Herbie said. King Ermine and Queen Ruby ruled the Land of Cloudy Skies.

"Hooray!" everyone whooped.

"Her name's Princess Pearl," Herbie told them.

Willow jumped up. "We should take her some presents."

"Us burrowing animals can dig down into the earth and find gold and jewels for her," piped up Marmaduke Mole.

"What a brilliant idea!" cried Willow. "Let's start digging."

The rabbits, moles, foxes and badgers began to burrow. Soon they had disappeared underground in a shower of snow and mud.

"Why don't the rest of us animals dig up fir and holly trees and plant a winter garden for the new princess?" Rory Weasel suggested.

"And dog roses," added Wendy Wood Mouse. "Their red hips are lovely at this time of year!"

"I know where some early snowdrops are growing," said Daisy Squirrel eagerly, her fluffy tail twitching. "A garden will be a brilliant present for a princess!"

The mice, weasels and squirrels scampered off in search of plants.

"What can *we* take Princess Pearl?"

Jemima asked the other birds.

Everyone thought hard, but nobody could come up with an idea.

"The sky's so empty in winter," sighed Isabella, at last. "It won't be easy to find anything."

"Let's all search for a present for the baby," said Jemima, "and meet back here at nightfall."

She took off and sped above the woods, looking out for something special for Princess Pearl. The cloudy sky stretched on and on, grey and empty. Below her, the trees were bare.

At last, when the clouds began to darken, she flew back to the pond and found the other birds in a gloomy huddle.

"Any luck, Jemima?" asked Suki.

Jemima shook her head.

"We didn't find anything, either," Gus said. "And the animals have already left for the palace with their plants and jewels."

"We should go, too," Jemima said, "or the baby will be in bed when we get there."

"We can't go without a present!" exclaimed Herbie. "Not when everyone else is taking something."

"Let's search on the way," said Jemima, fluttering up into the air. "Come on, everyone!" She could hardly wait to see the new princess.

The birds flew low over the darkening woods as they headed for the palace. Jemima flapped her wings hard to keep up with her bigger friends – she wasn't going to be left behind.

They soon spotted Willow, Marmaduke and the other burrowing animals up ahead. They were carrying mounds of gold and sparkling jewels.

"I wish there were jewels in the sky," cawed Ralph.

A little further on, they passed Rory, Wendy and the other animals laden down with plants for Princess Pearl's garden.

"Why didn't *we* think of giving the baby a garden?" groaned Isabella.

Then they spotted the lights of the palace ahead. "We're nearly there," Suki twittered anxiously.

Jemima thought about the sun, moon and stars that were hidden behind the clouds. Perhaps other things were hidden there, too … things that they could give to Princess Pearl.

"I'll fly up through the clouds and find something," she said.

"It's too high, Jemima," warned her friends.

"Not for me," Jemima replied determinedly. "I'll find a present and meet you all at the palace."

She flew through the dark sky – much higher than she'd ever been before – her wings beating fast. Soon they began to ache, but she wasn't giving up. She had to find a present for Princess Pearl.

Finally, Jemima reached a cloud. It was wet, cold and a dismal blacky-grey. "Here goes," Jemima said to herself. Taking a deep breath, she ducked inside.

Up, up, up she flew. Her feathers were soon soaking wet, but she struggled on. There was no way she was going back now! The stars might be only a few wingbeats away.

At long last she spotted a glimmer of light above her. It was very faint, but it gave her the strength to go on. "Nearly there," she

panted, flapping her wings harder than ever.

And then she was through the cloud. The sky was purply-blue, and silver stars twinkled all around. "Oh!" Jemima gasped. "Herbie was right. Stars are beautiful!" She gazed at them, open-beaked in wonder.

If only Princess Pearl could see them, she thought. *That would be the perfect present for her.*

Suddenly she had an idea. Taking one last look at the stars, Jemima raced back down to find her friends.

They had almost reached the palace. "Come quick!" Jemima cried. "I've found a present, but I need your help."

She flew up to the clouds again and her friends darted after her.

"Take hold of the edge of the cloud," said Jemima. "And pull as hard as you can."

The birds gripped the cloud with their beaks. Jemima caught hold of it, too. It was wet and cold and it tasted of snow. She began to fly backwards, tugging it with all her might. Her friends pulled just as hard.

At first nothing happened, then, slowly, the cloud began to move and a tiny gap appeared. Jemima could see a few stars glittering. "Keep pulling!" she said with her beak full of cloud.

They pulled harder than ever.

"Follow me, Isabella and Gus!" cried Herbie. "We'll shift that cloud over there."

Puffing and panting, the birds dragged the clouds apart until, at last, the sky was clear. Thousands of silver stars twinkled brightly.

"Amazing!" Suki gasped. "Well done, Jemima!"

"Well done, all of us," said Jemima. "Princess Pearl will love seeing this." She flew down to the palace. Rory Weasel and the other animals were hard at work planting the princess's garden. All around them, the snow was gleaming with beautiful, silver starlight, but they were so busy they hadn't noticed.

Jemima flew quickly round the palace, peeping in at the windows until she spotted the baby. She was lying in a cradle, playing with a gold rattle. Jemima tapped on the glass with her beak, then settled on the sill to see what would happen.

Queen Ruby came to the window. Her eyes widened in astonishment as she noticed the garden the animals were making. Throwing open the window, she leaned out to see better. She turned to King Ermine. "Come and look, my dear! And bring Princess Pearl."

King Ermine lifted the baby out of her cradle and hurried to the window. "Wonderful!" he exclaimed, holding the princess up so she could see the new plants.

"Look up!" chirped Jemima. "Look at the sky, Your Majesties."

The king and queen were still gazing at the garden, but Princess Pearl looked up at the stars. Cooing with delight, she stretched out her chubby arms towards them.

The little bird felt a thrill of excitement. It was clear the baby loved her present.

Now Jemima noticed that the burrowing animals had arrived at the palace.

"The animals have brought jewels," cried Queen Ruby.

"Thank you," called King Ermine. "Thank you for bringing those beautiful jewels and for planting such a pretty garden."

"Look up!" Jemima tweeted impatiently.

Willow, Marmaduke and the other burrowing animals halted on the palace steps and gazed, spellbound, at the starry sky. The animals in the new garden were staring at the stars, too. So were all the birds, who were perched on the castle's high walls.

"What are they all staring at?" asked Queen Ruby. She glanced up at the sky and

gasped in astonishment. "Ermine, look!" she exclaimed.

"Oh!" At last King Ermine spotted the twinkling stars. "How wonderful!"

Princess Pearl clapped her tiny hands.

"Now the clouds have gone, I will change the name of the kingdom," announced King Ermine. "From now on, it will be called the Land of Silver Stars."

Jemima flew across to join the others. "You found the perfect present for the baby, Jemima," said Gus.

"It's not just for Princess Pearl," Jemima replied. She looked round at her friends, who were still entranced. "Uncovering the stars has turned out to be a present for everyone."

THE
STAR WISH

Karen Wallace

Morgan was a monkey who was brown as a nutmeg. He had a cream face and white fur on his stomach. He lived with his mother and sister in a hot, leafy jungle where the trees were tall and grew thickly together. There were lots of monkeys in Morgan's family, but the oldest and the cleverest was called Plato and he was Morgan's grandfather.

While Morgan's sister Mango played with the other monkeys, Morgan went to see Plato. He swung over the pond in the clearing and through the branches of three trees until he came to the tree where Plato lived. Then he sat and listened to his grandfather's stories about when he was a star in a travelling circus.

One day, Plato told Morgan about how they had stopped in a mountain village covered with snow.

"What's snow?" asked Morgan.

Plato lifted Morgan on to his shoulders and climbed up to the very top of his tree. He pointed far away to where the mountaintops were white. "That's snow," he said. He patted Morgan's head. "It falls from the sky when it gets cold, and every snowflake is as tiny as a star at night."

Morgan stared at the mountains with wide eyes. "There must be *millions* of snowflakes," he said.

"Billions," said Plato. "And the amazing thing is that each one is different from the others."

"What do they feel like when they fall on your nose?" asked Morgan.

Plato laughed. "Cold and zingy!" he replied.

Morgan tried to imagine such a thing, but it was impossible. "Does snow ever fall in our jungle?" he asked.

Plato shook his head. "Hardly ever," he said.

Morgan's face fell. "I wish I could see snow," he murmured.

"Cheer up," said his grandfather. "You can always make a star wish."

"A star wish," repeated Morgan in a puzzled voice. "What's that?"

"You make a wish when you see a falling star," said Plato. He patted Morgan's head and smiled. "A star wish always comes true. Now, come along, it's bedtime."

Morgan watched his grandfather climb down, but he didn't move. He stared at the snow-capped mountains until it was almost too dark to see. Then one by one the stars began to come out.

As Morgan swung through the branches back to his own tree, he kept looking up, hoping to see a falling star. Luckily, he knew the way so well he didn't bump into anything. Then the most wonderful thing happened.

Morgan was swinging through the big tree over the pond in the clearing, when he saw a sparkling star fall through the night sky. Before he had a chance to make a wish, it disappeared and all Morgan heard was the tiniest *splash*.

The star must have fallen into the pond!

Morgan dropped through the branches as quickly as he could.

If he could catch the star before it sank, he could make his special wish for snow.

At first Morgan couldn't see any trace of his star in the pond, then he noticed a ring of ripples coming from a lily pad and saw something sparkling in the water.

Now Morgan knew that it was very dangerous for a monkey to come down from the trees near the edge of the pond. His mother had told him time and time again about the leopard that lived in the jungle, and how he always came down for a drink at night before he went out hunting.

And the problem with leopards was that you could never see them or hear them because they were so quiet and so clever.

But Morgan forgot everything he'd been told. Tonight was different. He had a star to find and a star wish to make!

He climbed down the tree and crept up to the edge of the pond. The sparkling thing was still under the lily pad. Now all he had to do was think of a way to get it out of the water.

Just then, a hard, horny paw grabbed his tail.

"Silly monkey!" cried his mother crossly. "I've been looking for you everywhere! What on earth do you think you're doing? A leopard will eat you for supper." And before

Morgan could say another word, his mother began to tug at his tail to take him home.

A few minutes later, Morgan was curled up beside his sister Mango. But he was so excited he couldn't sleep. More than ever, he was determined to get his star.

The next day at dawn, Morgan ran back to the pond, but the sparkling star had disappeared. With a heavy heart, he went to see his grandfather and told him the whole story.

"Of course you couldn't see your star," explained Plato. "Imagine the pond is a mirror. What you saw was a *reflection* of a star." He tickled Morgan's chin kindly.

"And stars only shine at night."

"But I saw the star fall out of the sky," cried Morgan. "And I heard it go *splash!*"

"Most likely a frog," grunted his grandfather. Then his voice went serious. "Even so, imagine if you had met a leopard!"

But Morgan didn't care about leopards. He was sure that a real star had dropped into the pond by the lily pad.

That night, when his mother and Mango were asleep, Morgan crept down the tree and made his way back to the pond in the clearing.

He crept along the edge until he found the lily pad. Then he pulled out a long reed and waggled it in the mud. A moment later, something sparkly glittered in the water.

It was his star!

Crack! A twig snapped in the darkness and the smell of leopard filled Morgan's nose. Every hair on his back stood up and his heart banged like a drum! His mother was right. It was too dangerous for a monkey to be in the jungle at night.

Morgan turned and ran home as fast as he could.

The following morning, Morgan made a plan. He was determined to lift the star out of the pond, but he had to do it quickly before the leopard had a chance to creep up on him.

He wove a net out of dry grass and tied it to the end of a strong stick.

"What's that net for?" asked Mango, hanging down from their tree by her tail.

"Catching butterflies," said Morgan.

Mango looked at him hard. "Fibber," she said, taking a bite of a papaya. "Since when have you been interested in butterflies?"

Morgan looked at his feet. He was never any good at making things up. "The truth is, I need your help," he said.

"What for?" asked Mango, narrowing her eyes.

"To make a star wish," said Morgan reluctantly.

"What's that?" demanded Mango.

"If I tell you my wish, it won't come true," said Morgan. He took a deep breath and grinned at his sister. "Come with me tonight and help me watch out for leopards."

Mango rolled her eyes. "No way," she said, and blew a mouthful of pips past his right ear. "You're crazy."

As soon as the sun had set, Morgan picked up his net and went back to the pond. This time he could clearly see the star in the water.

Morgan wanted to shout with joy! He remembered how Mango had called him crazy. Now he couldn't wait to see her face when his star wish came true and the jungle turned white.

Morgan wrapped his tail round a branch and leaned over the pond. Then he eased the star into the net and laid it on the grass.

The star was the most wonderful thing that Morgan had ever seen. Every part of it shimmered!

Suddenly, Morgan felt the leopard sitting beside him! This time he hadn't even heard a twig snap.

He opened his mouth to shout out with terror, but to his surprise, Morgan realized he wasn't frightened of the leopard.

It was as if they were both under the spell of the star.

The leopard turned his head and looked at Morgan. His yellow eyes were full of amazement. He stared at the star a moment longer, then he walked away.

When Morgan looked back down at the star, he saw it was falling apart. He made his wish and put it back in the pond as quickly as he could.

As the star sank in the dark water, it crumbled into a thousand pieces and Morgan imagined they were snowflakes falling in the night.

The first thing Morgan noticed as he awoke early the next morning was that everything was quiet. Usually the jungle was filled with the chatter of monkeys and the squawking of birds.

Morgan opened his eyes.

There was snow on the ground and snow on the branches. Snowflakes were falling out of the sky!

 Morgan felt a snowflake land on his nose. It was cold and zingy, just as Plato had said. "Yippeeee!" he shouted.

"Shush," muttered Mango, who was half asleep beside him. "Why are you shouting?"

Morgan shook his sister by the arm. "Open your eyes!" he cried. "My wish has come true. The jungle has turned white!"

Within seconds, all the other monkeys

awoke. "What's this white dust?" they hooted.

"It's not dust! It's *snow*," said Morgan. "My star wish came true."

"Wow!" cried the other monkeys as they swung down from their trees. "You're brilliant, Morgan!"

"I helped," yelled Mango. "He couldn't have done it without me!" But nobody was listening. They were too busy playing in the snow.

As for Morgan, he felt so pleased and so proud, he thought he would explode. Then he did what he had been planning to do from the moment he'd made his wish by the pond.

He made a fat, fluffy snowball and hit Mango right on her nose!

TIGER, THE
NO-GOOD
GUARD DOG

Malachy Doyle

Willow lived on a farm, high in the rolling
hills. One winter's morning, with the frost
sparkling on the windowpanes and the
duck pond frozen hard, Pa came in from
feeding the hens.

"There's been a fox in the yard," he said.

"Not again!" said Ma. "We're going to
have to do something about it."

"He didn't get into the chicken hutch,
did he?" asked Willow. She knew that

winter was a hungry time for foxes, and that chickens were one of their favourite foods.

"Not yet, love," replied Pa. "But he's a big fellow, by the look of his prints in the snow. If he set his mind to it, I'd say he'd find a way in there, no bother. What we need is a guard dog! One that will sleep outside in the yard, and bark when anything comes."

"Let's get a puppy!" said Willow. "Please, Pa! Please, Ma! We could get one from the dogs' home in town. It can be an early Christmas present, if you want. You won't have to get me anything else!"

"Hmmm." Pa wasn't too sure. "I'd rather get a fully grown, ready-trained dog. But if

we could find one that's right..."

"...then we could have a puppy!" cried Willow, running over and hugging him.

"Let's try it," said her mother, smiling at Pa. "As long as we pick a puppy that's sensible and strong, I'm sure you could train it up, dear."

Pa spent the rest of the day making a kennel, with a bit of help from Willow once she got home from school. And the next day was Saturday, so the two of them went out and bought all the things you need for a dog – food, a lead, a bowl, a brush and a ball.

Then they went off to the local dogs'

home. They looked at big dogs and small ones, fat ones and thin ones, young ones and old ones, friendly ones and shy ones.

Some of them Willow liked. Some of them Pa liked. But there wasn't one that they both liked and that looked as if it would make a good guard dog for the farm.

"Haven't you any puppies?" Willow asked the Dog Lady. "That's what I really want."

"We don't have many coming in," said the woman. "People usually only get rid of dogs when they become too big for them to handle, or too expensive for them to feed. There is one little sweetie, though – he only came in the other day..." And she took them through to the back.

As soon as Willow saw the puppy, in a pen all on his own, she knew he was the one for her.  And as soon as the Dog Lady let him out, he ran over to Willow, wagged his tail and licked her.

"I think he's got a bit of sheepdog in him," said the lady. "Look at his perky ears!"

"He's got a bit of a lot of things, by the look of him," said Pa. "He's a proper pick and mix, if you ask me!"

"Oh, he's lovely!" cried Willow, bundling him up in her arms. "We can take him, can't we, Pa?" She was worried, though, that he'd think the funny little pup was too small and friendly to be a guard dog. "You'll grow up to be big and brave, won't you, Tiger?" For she already knew what name she wanted to give him – a big, brave, tigery sort of name!

Tiger wagged his tail and then he licked her, once again. And the Dog Lady, who really wanted the pup to find a good home, grinned at them all, saying, "Oh yes! I'm sure he'll be big and brave!"

"Hmmm," said Pa, looking from Willow to the pup. "I suppose we could give it a go."

So Tiger went home in the back of the car.

"He's a quiet little fellow, isn't he?" said

Pa, driving off. "I don't know how that woman puts up with all the yapping in that place!" For every single dog they'd seen in the home had either been barking or whining. In fact, the only one that hadn't made any noise at all was Tiger.

When they got back to the farm, Pa opened the boot, and the little pup jumped out, bounded across the yard and ran straight into the house.

"What a sweet little pup!" said Ma as he jumped up and licked her.

"You can't stay in here, I'm afraid, little fellow!" said Pa, with a laugh. "You have to live outside in your kennel and bark when anyone comes – especially the fox!"

"But it's snowing!" said Willow.

"He'll be frozen!"

"He'll be fine, love," said Pa. "It's a big strong kennel and he's a fine healthy pup. If we let him sleep in the house, even for one night, it'll be much harder to get him to go outside."

So Willow took Tiger outside to show him his kennel.

"You're going to have to sleep out here, I'm afraid," she said. "Will you be all right, little one?"

Tiger gave her a sad sort of look, but he made his way into the very back of his new home, and lay down on the straw that Pa had put there for him.

Later, with the stars twinkling in the frosty
night, Willow sneaked out into the snowy
yard.

"Tiger?" she whispered at the door of
the kennel, and the pup came scampering
over to see her. "Here, look, I brought a nice
cosy blanket for you. But don't tell anyone
– it's our little secret!"

She crawled inside to give him a cuddle,
but she was so cosy in there, all wrapped up
in the blanket with her lovely new puppy dog,
that ten whole minutes
went by without her
even noticing.

"Willow! Are
you out there?"
It was her mother

134

at the door of the farmhouse.

"It's all right, Ma!" said Willow, scrambling to her feet. "I'm just saying goodnight to Tiger."

So Tiger lived in the yard and every time someone came to the gate, he raced over to see who it was. But he didn't bark and he didn't bite – no, he was such a friendly little dog that all he did was wag his tail and lick them!

"That fox has been back," said Pa, coming into the house early one morning. "I saw his footprints in the snow again. It's only a matter of time before he finds a way into the chicken run."

"Oh dear," said Ma. "And Tiger didn't bark?"

"Tiger never even growls," said Pa. "I'm doing my best to train him, but he's just too friendly! I'm sorry, Willow," he said, "but I'm going to have to take him back to the dogs' home and see if they've got something a bit fiercer."

"No, Pa!" cried Willow. "Please give him another chance! He's only learning!"

Pa looked from Willow to Tiger. "All right," he said, with a sigh. "We'll keep him till Christmas. But if he hasn't shown by then that he's got it in him to be a good guard dog…"

He shook his head then, and everyone knew what he meant.

On the night before Christmas, through the silence and the snow, came a stranger. But it wasn't the fox this time, and it wasn't Father Christmas, either.

The man climbed over the gate, then up a drainpipe and eased open an upstairs window. Then he crept into Ma and Pa's bedroom, and stole Ma's gold ring!

"Don't bark, dog!" hissed the burglar, on his way back out of the window again. For there was Tiger, right below him, wagging his tail. "Good dog," he whispered, dropping down to the snowy ground and hurrying across the yard. But Tiger chased after him.

The burglar didn't realize that Tiger only wanted to stop him and lick him. He thought, instead, that the little dog was trying to catch him. He thought he was going to *bite* him. So the burglar started running as fast as he could. But the yard was all icy and soon he was slipping and sliding. And Tiger, running even faster, got caught up in the burglar's legs.

"Stupid dog!" yelled the man, tumbling forward on to the frozen pond, which he hadn't even noticed because of all the snow. Sliding across it, unable to stop himself, he came to the thinner ice in the middle and crashed right through.

"Help!" he yelled. "Help! Help!"

"Wuff!" barked the excited little dog for the very first time in his life. "Wuff wuff!"

"What's that noise?" cried Willow, running into her parents' room. "It's Tiger, barking! There must be something wrong!"

And she ran downstairs, followed by Pa, followed by Ma. And there, by the light of the midwinter moon, they saw the little pup at the side of the pond, barking away.

And there, floundering around in the icy water, was the burglar.

"We can keep Tiger now, can't we, Pa?" said Willow as the shivering thief was led away, wrapped in a blanket. "He's proved that he's a good guard dog, hasn't he?"

Pa looked from Willow to Tiger. "I suppose we can," he said with a laugh. "I suppose he must be."

Tiger wagged his tail, then he licked him, then he yapped.

"And you've found your voice, haven't you, you clever little dog!' said Willow, picking Tiger up and hugging him.

And from that day on, Tiger always

barked when a stranger or a fox came into the yard. So Pa was happy, Ma was happy, and Willow was the happiest of all.

CATCH A FALLING STAR

Caroline Pitcher

Nakkertok was a young narwhal, which is a kind of small whale. His skin was blue-grey, and he had a sharp tusk, like a sea unicorn. His name meant "travel swiftly", because Nakkertok was the fastest in his family pod.

They had been racing. Nakkertok had sped under the ice like a shiny torpedo until he was in the lead, but he had swum so far ahead he'd become separated from the others.

Now he was lost.

"They're nowhere to be seen. I'm all alone in the ocean," he sighed. The ice stretched above him, as clear and shiny as a mint. Nakkertok knocked on it with his twisty tusk. *Tap, tap! Tap, tap!*

His tusk was really a tooth that grew up from near his mouth. It looked like a long stick of white barley sugar and it was very clever. It could tell him how thick the ice was, if the sea was too salty, when the water was beginning to freeze, where there were shoals of fish to eat, and who was swimming nearby.

Tap, tap! Nakkertok listened.

No one knocked back.

"*I* know! I'll call to them." He whistled.

No answer. He clicked and listened again, but still there was no answer. The vast Arctic Ocean lay in silence all around him.

"Ah! Maybe they're swimming below me, near the ocean bed," he cried. "I'll take some good big breaths at the top, and then I'll dive down and find them."

Narwhals can dive better than most sea creatures, and once Nakkertok had filled up with with air at the surface, he dived far deeper than he ever had.

The water darkened as he travelled towards the ocean bed. It became as gloomy as night. There were strange-looking fish he'd never seen before. One even carried its own lantern hanging from a little rod on its nose, as if it were fishing.

As Nakkertok swam eagerly towards the pretty light, he caught sight of a smaller fish swimming up ahead, lured by the bright glow. At once, the bigger fish's jaws opened and *snap!* the poor fish was gone. In dismay, Nakkertok realized that the strange fish was only waving its pretty little light to trap its supper.

For a while, Nakkertok searched the depths of the ocean, but it was eerily cold and quiet. There were no whales or dolphins sending songs and messages to each other. Nakkertok longed to hear the whistles and clicks and echoes from the others in his pod, but there was only silence.

And what was *that*? On the ocean floor lay what looked like a large cage. It was the

wreck of a ship that had sunk a hundred years earlier. Now green and red seaweed clung to the wreck, and softened its wooden ribs. Little fish darted in and out of its sad bones. Nakkertok fancied darting in and out, too, but he was wary of swimming inside, especially when he was alone. Supposing it closed round him and he couldn't get out again? He'd be trapped in that murky water forever.

He swam as near as he dared and knocked on the wreck's wooden bones. *Tap, tap!* It felt hard and *old*.

Nakkertok sensed something moving through the water, and heard a low call that sounded familiar. A creature was approaching, slowly, steadily. He realized that it was some kind of whale, but it was not a narwhal.

It was much, much bigger.

The creature loomed over the other side of the shipwreck. It was huge, and it had some bright, pale patches. Narwhals have pale skin when they are older and Nakkertok's blue-grey patches would turn paler in time, but this whale was black with white patches.

It was black with white patches because it was a *killer whale*!

"What now?" Nakkertok panicked. He turned and swam upwards, faster than he ever thought he could, away from the wreck, away from the danger, on through the water as it got lighter and lighter towards the surface.

His luck was in. The ice there had broken up. Nakkertok crashed through the waves, throwing water up all around him. With his heart pounding, he breathed in deeply, and swam on fast, hoping there was no killer whale chasing after him.

This time Nakkertok had got away, but oh, how he hated being all by himself. How was he ever going to find his pod? He dared not whistle to them in case that killer whale detected the sound, and came chasing after him for its supper.

The sea glittered around him and ice floes drifted like ghost ships. Nakkertok swam on to make sure he had escaped from the killer whale, and to search for his pod.

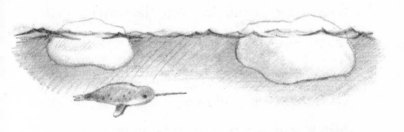

When he began to feel sleepy from all this swimming, he spun over on to his back. There he stayed, belly up. It was good to

rest for a while and rock gently on the cold, clear sea as if it was a cradle.

"Ahoy down there, young narwhal!" called a voice.

Nakkertok looked up and saw a great albatross soaring far above on wide wings. Nakkertok was pleased to see him. The albatross had circled the world, flying thousands of miles over the oceans. He must have experienced many different things and become a wise bird.

Nakkertok called, "Ahoy up there, Mister Albatross! Can you see a lot of the ocean when you're so high up in the sky?"

"Yes, I can," said the albatross, flying in a little lower. "I can see for miles and miles."

"Can you see any narwhals? As well as me, of course!"

The albatross circled above a little longer. Then he replied, "No. I'm afraid I can't see any at the moment. But you narwhals travel so fast, a pod may suddenly come speeding into view. You look so sad, young narwhal. What has happened?"

"We were racing and somehow I got too far ahead and was separated from all the others," cried Nakkertok, "and I may never see my pod again!"

"Don't be so sad and downhearted, young one," called the albatross. "I'm sure you'll

find each other again, somewhere, some day. It's just that the ocean is so very big – I should know! Look on the bright side. I've always found my way by looking at the stars. And I've often found that something special happens in the sky at night. Some kind of magic. Just you wait, and watch, and see!"

The albatross wheeled away on his solitary journey over the ocean.

Nakkertok watched him for as long as he could, until he felt sleepy and his small eyes closed.

Nakkertok dozed for a while. When he woke, at first he thought he was still with his pod of narwhals. Full of hope, he looked all around him. There was no one.

"Oh, now I remember," he sighed. "I'm all alone. I may never see my pod again. But I do feel a little better for that sleep. And, oh wow, just look at that sky!"

The sky had changed while he had slept. It was no longer the vivid ultramarine blue of daytime. Night was here. Nakkertok was lying under a great dark dome that shimmered with stars. There were so many that they almost hid the blackness with their icy-white twinkling. Nakkertok blinked up at the dazzling dome and watched the bright sky, spellbound. It was so beautiful that he felt full of hope again. Maybe he *would* find his pod, somewhere, some day.

"Mister Albatross told me, *Look on the bright side.* Well, it's certainly all bright up there!" cried Nakkertok. The stars shimmered and twinkled, and as he watched, one of them began to tumble out of the sky, leaving a thin trail of sparkling dust behind it, like gossamer, as it fell into the sea.

Some kind of magic? Quick! Catch it if you can!

Nakkertok slipped under the waves and sped through the ice floes to where he thought the bright star would land. His heart pounded as he swam faster and faster, until he was right underneath the falling star, just before it hit the water. It landed on his tusk.

At the very same time, he heard a chorus of voices he knew so well, calling,

"Nakkertok! At last we've found you. Where have you been? We've been searching for you everywhere!"

It was the dearest sound in the world to him. The other narwhals of his pod came plunging and leaping joyfully through the sea towards him.

"We saw the falling star and raced to catch it before it landed in the sea," cried his sister. "And you reached it first,

Nakkertok. You're always the fastest! But the falling star has brought us back together again, and that's wonderful."

The star pulsed and shone like a little silver heart on the very tip of Nakkertok's tusk.

Nakkertok shook it gently so that it trembled. Then he threw the star right back up into the sky and there it stayed, twinkling among the other stars.

"You're back where you belong, safe and happy, star," said Nakkertok. "And so am I!"

MIKI'S MAGICAL SLEIGH RIDE

Caroline Juskus

It was a crisp, white Arctic morning and Sura was excited. Today was Christmas Eve!

"Morning!" she chirruped brightly to her pa's sleeping huskies.

A young pup wagged his tail and jumped up to lick her cheeks.

"Hello, Miki," laughed Sura. "Now I shan't have to wash! Which gives me more time to prepare the sleigh!"

She was spending Christmas with her cousin, Chu, and it would be a long trek to get there. Shivering, she looked out across the freezing tundra. The sun was shining and the snow glistened, but the air was biting cold. The dogs stirred in their nests of snow and shook out their thick fur coats. Sura harnessed them to the front of the sleigh and Miki waited eagerly. He'd never pulled a sleigh before, but he'd been dreaming of it since the day he'd been born.

"Sorry, Miki," said Sura, stroking him softly. "I'm afraid it's too long a journey for you."

Miki's ears drooped and the young girl gave him a hug. She knew how desperate he was to pull the sleigh. "Don't worry,"

she said. "You'll get your chance very soon. There's a kind old man called Santa who brings presents at Christmas and I've asked him for something very special. Something we can share. I think you're going to love it!"

Miki cheered up and ran in a circle, chasing his tail. Sura pointed to his tracks. "See those?" she said. "You'll be ready to join the main pack when your pawprints are as big as the other dogs'."

Miki looked at his pawprints and was about to ask his mum how long it would take for them to grow when his master arrived. Like Sura, he was dressed from head to toe in warm furs, and his arms were brimming with bags and boxes.

"Food for the Christmas feast!" he told Sura as he piled the luggage on to the sleigh. "If you're good, there might be some presents, too! On you hop."

Sura laughed. "But there's hardly any room!" she exclaimed. She had to have two bags on top of her knees and so it was with great difficulty that she gave Miki one last hug. "Couldn't Miki come with us?" she asked hopefully. "He could sit on my lap."

"I think your lap's already full!" teased her father. "And I'm afraid we've a heavy load as it is. But our neighbour is going to keep her eye on him and I've left him some tasty treats!"

Miki gave Sura a lick and then scampered over to his mum.

"Don't worry, little Miki," his mum whispered. "Someone is going to take care of you and we'll be back very soon."

"Do you promise?" yapped Miki, trying to be brave.

"I promise," said his mum, nuzzling his cheek. "Now go and take a look by the house. The master has left you your favourite food. Walrus meat. Eat it all up, and you'll be big and strong by the time I get home."

Just at that moment the master called, "Yup, yup, yup!" and the huskies pulled at the reins, panting eagerly. It was the signal they'd been waiting for.

"Bye, Miki," called Sura. "I'm going to miss you. Make a deep nest next to the house. It's sheltered there, and you'll keep cosy and warm."

"Yip," barked Miki sadly.

Miki's mum gave him one last reassuring tail wag, and then the sleigh vanished over the snowy horizon. Glumly, Miki returned to the house and as he did, his nose picked up the delicious scent of walrus meat. He felt a little better as he tucked into the tasty treat. Then, with a full belly, he dug a deep nest and soon fell fast asleep.

Miki was so warm and cosy that it was many hours before he woke up. The sky had turned black and was glimmering with hundreds of silver stars. His ears pricked up. He could hear the sound of a man's voice! Had his master come back? Bushy-tailed, Miki ran to find him.

But it wasn't his master. It was an old man in a red suit. He was talking to a team of reindeer harnessed to his sleigh. *That's odd*, thought Miki. *I didn't know reindeer pulled sleighs.* He noticed that the lead reindeer was holding one of his legs awkwardly and the old man was examining it.

"Poor Rudolph," the man said kindly. "I'm afraid you'll have to rest up. You won't be able to fly tonight."

Fly! thought Miki. He couldn't believe his ears. "Excuse me," he barked before he could stop himself, "but did you say your reindeer can *fly?*"

The old man turned. "Hello, little fellow," he said. "Who are you?"

"I'm Miki," yapped Miki.

"I'm Santa," said the man in a jolly voice.

Miki cocked his head in amazement. Incredibly, the old man seemed to have understood everything he'd said! Not even Sura could do that.

"These are my special flying reindeer that help me deliver presents to all the

children round the world," Santa continued.

"I was just delivering a present for Sura, but we had a bit of a slippery landing and Rudolph here has hurt his leg."

"Poor Rudolph," barked Miki.

"But Sura isn't here. She's gone to stay with her cousin, Chu."

"Oh dear," said Santa. "Then I don't know how I'm going to get her present to her. Or what to do about all the other boys and girls. I can't fly without Rudolph."

Miki didn't like the idea of Sura and all the other children not getting their presents. "I could help you!" he yapped. "I could pull your sleigh!"

"You?" asked Santa.

"I've watched my mum. I'm sure I can do it."

"Well, in that case," chuckled Santa, "welcome to my team!"

Miki chased his tail in wild excitement. He was going to be pulling a sleigh at last!

"Thank you for helping us," chorused Santa's reindeer.

Miki beamed, then thought for a moment. "But what about Rudolph?" he asked.

"Rudolph just needs to rest," said Santa. "I'm sure he'll be better soon."

"He can stay in my nest!" said Miki. "That will keep him warm and cosy."

Santa unharnessed the lame reindeer from the front of the sleigh, and Miki made his nest bigger. Rudolph tried it out for size. "It's perfect," he said. "Now I can have a lovely sleep."

Santa adjusted Rudolph's harness and buckled Miki in. It was then that Miki remembered that this was no ordinary sleigh. It was a *flying* sleigh. "Oh dear," he said. "I'm not sure I can fly." He tried jumping, but he couldn't stay up in the air.

"Ho, ho, ho," chuckled Santa. "My magic will soon sort that."

"Magic?!" yapped Miki.

"Close your eyes," said Santa as he showered Miki with silver dust.

Miki's paws tingled. Then something

truly magical happened – his paws lifted off the ground! When he opened his eyes he could barely believe it. He was soaring over Sura's house! "I'm flying!" he spluttered.

"You're a natural," said Santa. "Now we need to find Sura and deliver her present."

Miki steered the sleigh towards the North Star, the bells on the sleigh jingling merrily, his thick coat keeping him warm as the chill wind whistled in his ears. He didn't know whether he'd picked up his mum's scent or if it was Santa's magic, but he was sure he was heading in the right direction.

Then the sky grew white with a flurry of snowflakes. Soon everything was coated in a fresh blanket of glistening snow and Miki grew worried that he'd never find Sura. He looked down to see he was flying over more rooftops. No lights shone from the windows and no smoke billowed from the chimneys for it was very late and everyone was in bed.

Suddenly, he spotted his mum and the rest

of the pack curled up by a log cabin! They were all asleep with their noses twitching. "I think we're here, Santa!" said Miki. "Look, Mum! It's me! I'm Santa's lead dog!" he cried.

"Don't wake them," hushed Santa. "Delivering Christmas presents is supposed to be kept secret."

"Oops, sorry!" whispered Miki.

The sleigh landed softly on top of the roof, and Santa unbuckled Miki's harness. "Want to help me give Sura her present?" he asked, pulling it from his sack.

"Yes, please!" yapped Miki.

Miki and Santa sneaked down the chimney into a small room lit by the lights of a Christmas tree. Miki chased his tail in excitement and let out another yap.

ON A
Starry
NIGHT

"Hush," Santa reminded him as they left Sura's present beneath the tree, along with a present for her cousin.

Upstairs in her cousin's room, Sura stirred. She was sure she'd just heard a dog yap and it sounded just like Miki! She sat up in bed. "Did you hear something?" she whispered to Chu.

"It was probably just the wind," said her cousin sleepily.

But Sura knew it wasn't. Had her little pup followed their sleigh tracks? She slipped on her boots, skipped downstairs and ran outside, but there was only the pack of sleeping huskies and Miki wasn't with them. Sadly, she turned to go back to bed, but then a jingle overhead made her look up. There, to her astonishment, soaring through a sky of shimmering stars, was Santa. With a small grey-and-white dog leading his sleigh! A dog that looked very much like...

"Miki!" cried Sura. "Miki, is that you?"

She rubbed her eyes in disbelief and when she looked again, the sleigh had gone. She must have been dreaming. Sura made her way back inside the cabin and was about to climb the stairs when she noticed a pile of presents under the tree. And one of them had her name on it! Far too excited to wait until morning, she ripped off the paper and there inside was exactly what she'd asked for!

"Sura?" mumbled Chu, stepping into the room. "What are you up to?"

"Santa's been!" cried Sura. "Look, he's left me this!"

"What is it?" asked Chu.

"It's a sleigh," said Sura, "and it's just the right size for me to sit on and for my favourite little pup to pull. It's a shame Miki isn't here to see it, though."

"Are you *sure* he isn't here?" said Chu, looking at the floor. "Because then who do all these little pawprints belong to?"

Sura suddenly noticed a sooty trail leading from the fireplace to the Christmas tree. "You're right, they're Miki's prints!" she whooped. "I'd recognize them anywhere!" She pointed to a sooty circle. "Look, that's where he chased his tail. He always does that!"

"Then where is he now?" asked Chu.

"Pulling Santa's sleigh!" cried Sura.

She dashed back outside and looked up at the sky again. It was filled with nothing but twinkling stars, yet she knew he was still up there somewhere. "Happy Christmas, Miki!" she called. "You're the best pup ever!"

And from somewhere far away she was sure she heard a puppy yap, "Happy Christmas, Sura!"

THE
BRIGHTEST
STAR

Penny Dolan

Way down south, where the land of North America curves inwards, a lazy river spreads across flat marshlands, sliding its way to the sea. All winter, large families of snowgeese graze among the grass. In spring they set off on a great adventure.

Tumbler circled once more, feeling the wind under her wings. Then she flew down towards the marsh where her family lived.

"Here I come!" the young snowgoose called, folding in the ends of her wings.

Tumbler landed just beside Snowtail, her big sister, who moved over so that Tumbler could sit next to her. Stormboy, their brother, was paddling his webbed feet in the nearest mud.

Mother Snowgoose stretched her long white neck above the reedy grass to check on her three children. Only a year before they had been three eggs in a nest. Snowtail hatched first, Stormboy second and little Tumbler last of all.

Back then they were bundles of downy grey fluff. Now they wore white plumage,

their wings were tipped with long dark feathers, and they had handsome orange beaks and feet. Their small round eyes were alert and bright.

"How well they have grown!" Mother Goose was glad. Soon the great flocks of snowgeese would leave these marshes for the nesting grounds far away in the north.

That evening, as they all sat preening their feathers, she reminded them of the journey to come. "Listen, children," she said, "the sun is drying out the grassy marshes. Soon we must set off on the Great Journey Home. It will take many weeks."

"When? When?" the three young ones asked eagerly.

"Very soon!" said Father Goose, arriving in a flurry of feathers.

Tumbler felt worried. When they had flown south, Mother and Father had been beside them constantly. This time they would need to learn how to make the journey themselves, just in case they got separated from their parents.

"What if we get left behind by the other geese?" said little Tumbler nervously. "How will we know which way to fly?"

"I will tell you a secret," Father Goose said. "Each night the Great Star-Goose appears in the sky, heading north. His eye is the brightest star. So if you get lost, look for that shining star and fly to where the Great Star-Goose is pointing."

Tumbler liked that idea. It made her feel more confident about the long journey.

"You must try and keep together, too. Understood?" said Mother Goose. "Now eat!"

Peck, peck, peck! The three young snowgeese moved through the grass, gobbling down as much as they could. The flocks rarely stopped for food once they were migrating.

All around, snowgeese were cleaning their feathers and stretching their wings. The marsh was filled with hundreds of cries.

"Now? Now?"

"Soon! Soon!"

Each day the flocks of snowgeese waited.

Then, one dawn, the three young snowgeese heard the calls change.

"Fly! Fly!" the flocks were crying. "Time to go!" All around, birds were stretching their wings.

One, two, three, off! Up flew all the snowgeese, high into the sky. Soon the family was no more than five small spots among the blizzard of whirling wings. At first, the snowgeese made huge looping patterns in the air. Then they set off, following the vast river inland.

"Keep with me!" Stormboy called to his sisters. "We'll do it!"

On flew the flocks of snowgeese, on and on. Dusk came, then night, then another dawn. The birds flew onwards, day after day, hundreds of them. More joined the flock. Before long, there were thousands of snowgeese making the journey north. The three young snowgeese could no longer see their parents.

"Mother? Father?" called Tumbler anxiously.

From somewhere among the crowds of beating wings came her father's call, "Just keep going, little one. Follow the brightest star."

"I will, I will!" Tumbler flew as hard as she could, but she was very glad that Stormboy and Snowtail were flying close by.

"Keep going, Tumbler!" they called encouragingly.

After several days, the wilderness began changing. A week or so later, the snowgeese reached wide farmlands dotted with a few barns and farmhouses. Below lay vast fields bristling with corn stubble. Down among those stalks lay fat grains of corn.

"Food! Food!" the snowgeese called to each other, descending like a flurry of snowflakes.

"Over here, Tumbler," Snowtail cried, swooping towards the cover of a hedge where they searched hungrily for corn.

"There's more over there," Stormboy said, flying to where grain had been scattered all over the ground. It looked as if someone had left a feast for them. All he thought about was how good it was to gobble up the grains of corn! Snowtail and Tumbler stayed where they were, eating what they could find and keeping watch. Suddenly, they spotted something moving. Far off there were a few men with strange long sticks, made of metal that glinted in the sunlight.

The two sisters had the same desperate thought.

"Stormboy! Hunters!" they cried, warning their brother.

He heard their calls and flew low across the field towards them. The very next moment, the guns blasted out, again and again behind him.

"Oh!" Stormboy gasped. "Thank you."

The moment the terrible noise stopped, the three snowgeese flew fast into the air, before the hunters had time to reload their guns.

They soon caught up with the flocks of snowgeese. On they all flew, growing hungrier by the day. Sometimes they landed, ate whatever they found, and were off again, still heading north in search of their yearly nesting grounds.

However, this year, spring was late arriving and the air was still cold. The flock landed for a rest and found the ground almost covered by a blanket of bright white snow.

"Snow! Snow!" called Stormboy as they descended.

"Beautiful!" said Snowtail.

"White as our feathers," called Tumbler.

But, oh, what a disappointment it was! The snow was not soft like feathers. It was icy and too hard to break though. The snowgeese could not get to any grain. All they found were stale seeds and tough grass.

"I'm starving," said Stormboy.

"Me, too," added Snowtail.

Little Tumbler was too hungry to speak.

That night, the birds roosted by a deserted barn, fluffing up their feathers to keep themselves warm. Tumbler peered up at the starry sky, wondering if the Great Star-Goose ever got hungry.

A new day came. All across the feeding grounds, the snowgeese shivered, waiting for a change in the weather. At last the wind felt softer and all the snowgeese set off again, flying day after day, over rivers and ridges, snatching food and rest where they could.

By now, they were getting very tired.

"Are we nearly there yet?" Tumbler asked his sister and brother.

"Soon," said Stormboy.

"Quite soon," said Snowtail. "Just keep going."

Then came the moment when they saw an enormous city, full of tall towers and skyscrapers appearing on the horizon.

"Come on, you two," said Snowtail. "I remember flying over the city before. It will be easier, I promise."

As they flew over the miles of tall buildings and busy streets, the hot air rose up in streams, lifting the birds higher. Each wingbeat took the birds further than before and they glided along, resting their wide wings on the currents of warm air.

"This is fun," Stormboy called across to his sisters.

Soon, the long bay of the big city stretched ahead of them, with all its tiny boats bobbing about on the white-tipped waves.

Tumbler suddenly remembered something. "This is where we see the Green Lady!" she cried. "And there she is!"

Ahead, on an island in the middle of the water, stood the statue of a great Green Lady. She wore long coppery-green robes and a crown with seven spikes. Her strong right arm held up a golden flame, shining in the bright sunshine.

"Hello!" the three snowgeese called to her as they flew past.

It can't be far now, thought Tumbler to herself, worried about being left behind. "As long as we can reach the great forest, we will be all right."

"Onwards!" called the other snowgeese. "Onwards!"

They passed over the wide waterfall where water thundered down into a chasm, and rainbows danced in mist and spray.

"We flew across here on the way down, too, didn't we?" called Tumbler.

"We must be getting near home," Snowtail told them. "All we have to do now is keep up with the others." All was going well.

Then, one morning, a terrible storm came. The sky filled with swirling grey clouds and rain fell sharp as nails. Fierce winds picked up the three young birds, throwing them this way and that, no matter how hard they flew.

"Are you there?" Tumbler cried, beating her wings desperately. It was so dark she could hardly see.

"We're here," the other two called. "We're coming."

They struggled nearer until they were flying so close that their wingtips nearly touched. Now and again, lightning lit the clouds and the air shook with thunder. The birds' only thought was to keep going, no matter what or where.

Eventually, the storm passed. But where were the others? No friendly wings were beating nearby. No snowgeese were calling to them. There was only a vast pine

forest below, stretching for miles in every direction.

Night was coming on, there was nothing to mark their way and they felt hopelessly lost.

Tumbler found it so hard to keep up with her brother and sister. Wearily, she flew on. Bit by bit, she fell behind until they seemed like shapes far ahead, leaving her alone to face the night sky.

Sadly, Tumbler glanced up at the stars. They reminded her of something. Suddenly, she felt so much happier and flew so fast that she caught up with the other two.

"Don't worry!" said Tumbler. "Don't you remember what Father told us?"

"What?" they asked.

"The Star-Goose, of course!"

And there, like the eye of the great bird flying ahead of them, was the brightest star, showing them the way home.

On they flew. Before long they had left the forest far behind them. Ahead lay the familiar, flat green nesting grounds, crowded with thousands of snowgeese. Where were their parents?

"This way! This way!" Mother Snowgoose called to them from her nest among the mosses and grasses.

"We're here at last!" the three young snowgeese answered, as Father Snowgoose came flying up to meet them.

"Well done!" he said. "Well done, all of you."

Snowtail, Stormboy and Tumbler flew triumphantly in to land. Their Great Journey was safely over.

There, in the north of Canada, the three young snowgeese will live, making new families and maybe even hatching their own goslings. When summer ends and the wind is full of the scent of snow, all the snowgeese will rise in the air and fly all the way back south once again along the remembered routes.

Have you read…

WINTER
Magic

A Spellbinding Collection of Christmas Animal Tales

A Heart-warming Treasury of Animal Stories

WINTER
Wishes

A Magical Collection of Animal Tales